Cold As Ice

Cursed Heroes

BY: William D. Ollivierre

A MOW Universe Publishing Production
Published by William D. Ollivierre

ISBN: 978-1-7359149-5-4

I would like to thank God for bringing me from a ten-year-old child that could barely read or write, to allowing me to finish and publish book after book.

Also, thank my family and friends for all the support, I wouldn't be writing without it.

Last special thanks to Emoni McGregor for all the help getting this book ready.

For all those who need an escape from reality.

Come escape with me.

Cold As Ice

Cold As Ice

"It's been such a long day today. Sigh, you know I really hate this planet. Can you believe it has forty hours of daylight every day here? Plus, it only has 2 hours of night, how is anyone supposed to sleep around here?" Said Will, to his faithful companion, who just looked up at him as he continued to speak. "I always forget you can't talk. Thanks a lot brother, makes me the perfect sidekick and doesn't give it a voice box. Sometimes I think that guy just likes messing with us." He said as he looked down at the robotic spider, he held in his hands. "Well, my friend I think it's time we get going to that outpost. I think we should try getting to the next planet before the next sun starts to rise." He paused for a moment looking around. "Leave it to 24 to send me to the one-star system that has a small sun in orbit with the planets, orbiting around two blue giant stars." Will said looking his spider in the eyes. Oddly enough, despite looking like a real spider, it only had two eyes, which was because 24 found them creepy, so he made it with just two eyes so it would be less creepy.

Will smiled and stretched his hands into the air

above him yawing, then he put the spider on his shoulder, kicked his feet, and slid from the cliff he was sitting on. As he fell, he looked out over the area and spoke. *"Scan the area Two, find the best place for me to take off from, we need to leave for the next planet once it lines up with this one."* The small robotic spider attached a line to Will then launched itself a few feet above him to scan the area. Will opened his hands and legs to slow his fall as the spider beeped and hummed above him, a few seconds passed then the spider pulled itself back down. *"Looks like you're ready, Active Nannies .05 percent, relay the coordinates to me Two, it's time we get going."* *Will spoke as he fell faster, pulling his hands in and straightening out his body to fall straight down.*

His eyes changed color from a dark brown to a crystal-clear blue, and his breath turned white as it froze the air. He took a deep breath in, and just as he hit the ground, he took off seeming to vanish from the spot, a loud boom, and a large frost-covered crater was left where he landed. Within seconds, he had traveled four miles, landing in the middle of a valley outside of the mountains he had just jumped off. He looked around and vanished again, leaving behind a fifty-foot line of frozen grass heading in the direction he went. Seconds later, he appeared in an open valley that was surrounded by towering rock pillars. *"There, I see the base on the third planet coming into alignment."* Will spoke as he pointed up to the purple skies at a dim outline of one of the planets in the sky. *"Hold on Two, I'm going for it."* He said, staring at the sky.

He dropped down to one knee and placed one hand on the ground as he looked straight into the skies. *"Increase Nannie activation by .25% to .3% activation."* A white fog started falling from his body as the air around him grew ice cold. As the fog drifted off his body, it froze everything it touched, slowly creeping like a frozen hand turning everything it took hold of to ice. *"Just a few more seconds Two."* He spoke, dropping his head for a few seconds, then suddenly he pushed off the ground.

The ground shook, and a frozen shock wave rippled out from where he was. The doom from take-off echoed with the frozen wave, as it moved like the wind, freezing everything for nearly a mile in an instant. A white cloud could be seen going straight up, and a few seconds later, he was leaving the planet's atmosphere. The cloud that followed him disappeared as he moved out past the outer atmosphere and into space. He was right on target for the third planet in the system, flying like a comment threw the space between the two planets.

"Are we really going to try and fight that?" Said Sam as he pointed at Will flying through space. Sam is a crewman on board the Finder, a ship that was entering the system heading right for Will path. *"Do you have a death wish, we aren't here to assist in the battle. We are here to help get everyone out of his way."* Said the Captain of the ship as he changed course to follow behind Will, flying in close behind him like the tail of a comet. *"So, we aren't fighting by his side?"* Replied Sam. *"No boy, we don't even have weapons on this ship. Everything unnecessary was stripped out to make as much room as possible for this mission. All we have to do is get as many people as possible out of this system as fast as possible. Our sister ships will be coming to help us so just worry about that for now."* Said the captain to Sam. Sam didn't know much about space, seeing that this was his first time leaving his home system. Actually, it was the first

time he had even gone past the moon of the planet he was from.

Sam however, was very eager to show off what he could do. But picking up people and carrying them away was not what he had in mind for his great adventures in space. He had grand hopes of taking part in some great space battle, fighting off evil and being the hero that saves that planet, not being a glorified space taxi faring people off a world he had never heard of while running away from the battle.

"But why would you take out the weapons? What if we are needed to help… I mean… I thought this battle was going to be huge. There is no way one person could fight it alone." Said Sam with eagerness to fight. The Captain looked over at him and spoke. *"I guess they weren't lying when they told me you would be a hand full. Oh well, I guess I will have to explain some things, seeing that no one else told you how this works. That one man you see in front of us is called Will Number Two, he is a member of The Brothers Will. Not only that, but he is one of the top members having a single-digit number after his name. Which makes him what is known as a powerhouse*

member..." The Captain was cut off mid-sentence. *"Who are the Brothers Will, and why does it matter if he is a member of them?"* Sam asked, making the Captain a bit annoyed from him being cut off, but he just smiled and continued. *"Wow, you really don't know much about the universe outside of your homeworld, do you? I guess I have to explain who they are to. The Brothers Will are an alliance of some of the most powerful beings in the universe, their advanced technology, and undying bodies give them abilities that anyone else can only imagine. But what makes this one so special is his number Two rank, which means he is one of the most powerful members of the whole alliance."* Sam looked on with eager eyes as his captain continued to talk.

"All the members of The Brothers Will that have single-digit numbers as their rank are drifters, they travel from planet to planet, helping out the planet's people, but never staying more than a few hours so as not to damage the planet's ecosystem. But they never fight unless they are ordered to, which only happens if another member is defected."

The Captain pointed out of the window at Will.

Cold As Ice

"That right there is number Two the most powerful of the Power-house members, he is so powerful that to keep the planet stable his Nannies cool the atmosphere around him when active." Sam looked out at Will with wide eyes as he started to speak. *"Captain, what kind of spacesuit is he wearing? I can't tell from this far."* The Captain laughed, then answered his question. *"He isn't wearing one, most of the Brothers Will don't wear one, it just gets in their way. They don't actually need to breathe to stay alive, I actually don't know what they need to stay alive."*

"That's amazing, I didn't know there was anything that could live in space." Sam said, looking out of the cockpit window, his eyes glued to Will. The Captain laughed to himself, then continued talking. *"Well, first off I wouldn't call it living, it's more like just not dying, to be more accurate. Now get ready the funs about to start. We are going to fly into the planet's atmosphere ahead of him to clear the inhabitance of the planet."* The Captain placed his hands on the controls and spoke again. *"Get ready kid, it's time for us to go to work. Computer switch to manual controls."* Sam jumped forward, grabbed hold of the controls in front of him, as the Captain pushed the

throttle forward.

The Finder increased speed rapidly, moving around Will and leaving him behind as it headed straight to the planet below. Its engines roaring pushing the ship faster and faster. *"Now it's time you find out why this ship is called The Finder."* The Captain said as he looked over at Sam, pushing the throttle all the way forward. Pinning the two to their seats as the ship hurled through the outer atmosphere of the planet. *"Activate the sensors, let's see where everyone is."* The Captain said as he pointed to a button in front of Sam. Sam pushed the button, and the screen in front of him light up, dots appearing all over it, they were all different colors, and some were blinking. *"All those dots are groups of people on the planet. Our job is to pick up any group smaller than five. But we also have to mark each group for pick up that we aren't picking up, so they can be picked up by the larger ships that are on their way."* Said the Captain as he pointed out the dots on the screen, each color had a number showing how far away they were, green was close enough to pick up, red was too far to get a number count, and orange was close enough to mark but to large a group to pick up.

Cold As Ice

Then the ones that were blinking were ready to be locked onto and would stop once a lock was made.

The Captain let go of the throttle and grabbed hold of the steering controls in front of him. *"The secondary engines will be kicking in as soon as we reach the last layer of the atmosphere. When it does, I will need you to direct me to each group. You will be giving me the heading and distance, also whether we will be picking them up or just marking their location. That's where your job gets tricky, at the speed we will be moving, we will not have a choice of stopping to pick anyone up. So, you're going to have to teleport them on board safely. There will only be a ten-second gap from when they come into range to the time they are out of range. That's your one and only window we can't turn back. Last thing to remember, the larger ships do not have the sensors to pick up groups smaller than 50, so we have to mark every group we cannot pick up."* The Captain explained what they were going to be doing, and as he did the excitement could be heard in his voice. He was trying to hide it, but it was written all over his face, and it was obvious this wasn't his first time doing something like this.

Sam nodded his head and asked. *"How long do we have to get this done?"* The Captain clenched onto the controls and spoke. *"We have ten minutes before the first of the large transport ships will be entering the atmosphere, and one hour before Will hits the planet's atmosphere."* Sam looked back at the screen with all the dots. His mind racing, it was starting to set in. What he was about to be doing wasn't going to be as simple as picking a few people up and running away.

The ship started to shake as the secondary engines kicked in, then the screen in front of Sam started displaying distances next to the dots. *"25 degrees by 17 hours, 400 miles to pick up."* Sam shouted out, seeming to be more excited than before.

The Captain pulled on the controls, and the ship jerked as it changed directions and headed straight along the heading that Sam had just given. Sam looked at his controls, taking them in his hands, he was ready... He hoped. He had set a path straight through 40 large groups, though at this speed, he would only have two to three seconds to launch the markers for each group.

Cold As Ice

The clock was ticking as the ship flew across the planet at supersonic speeds, launching markers every few seconds as it passed by the large groups and transporting the small groups onboard into stasis pods in the ship's cargo bay. The minutes dragged on like unending hours as the ship flew through the skies.

The first wave of large ships started to enter the atmosphere one by one, each heading for the markers that were closest to their entry point. The clock was now ticking down even faster, and the real work was just getting started. Sam looked over at the Captain, who had a smile on his face gripping the controls tighter. The minutes ticked on, and more and more large ships showed up to transport the groups that had markers.

"Captain, I am sending you a path that I worked out to your monitor, you need to step on it, we don't have much time left before Will gets here." Said Sam as he sent over a map of the planet with a path to follow on it. "He was working on the map and directing the Captain at the same time, he might be a kid, but he was brilliant. No wonder he got recommend to be on my ship." The Captain thought as he pulled on the controls taking the

Cold As Ice

Ship along the path that was sent to his screen.

"I have a question for you Captain." Said Sam. *"Go ahead, ask away, I'll do my best to answer."* Replied the Captain. *"Well, it's just that you know a lot about the Brothers Will, and I don't. I'm just wondering if it's because I haven't traveled outside of my homeworld before. Or do you just know more about them than the average person?"* The Captain laughed as he pulled at the controls. *"You are a smart one to ask that question, I do know more about them than the average person. Actually, I would say I know more about them than anyone else that isn't a member."* Sam moved his controls as fast as he could to keep up, tagging all the groups as he spoke. *"Wow, so what makes you so special that you know so much more than everyone else?"* Asked Sam, fumbling over his words trying to keep up with the movement of the ship.

The Captain pulled back on the controls, and the ship went into a swirl. *"Hurry kid, you need to keep up. We don't have much more time. And the reason I am different is because I am the Captain that was in charge of the ship when Will 700 took it on his first mission to* save the world he now protects. 700 modified the engines in this ship to boost its power to allow us to get where we were going in the limited time we had, but it's what happened after that mission that made me different. After that mission, my crew went on to do other things and this ship was taken by Will 24. The modifications that Will 700 had made were not very safe. So much so that they were not supposed to be in the hands of a normal Captain. So, I agreed to work alongside them, in exchange, Will 24 upgraded my ship fully. Giving it more speed, better shields, and a set of very unique controls to help me control the upgrades. Since then, I have been traveling through the universe alongside the Brothers Will. I help get people to safety, delivering messages, and even transporting members from time to time. You may have noticed no one told you my name, and that's because I never use it anymore. Just like the Brothers Will that go by numbers, I just go by Captain now. I gave up my past with my name to do this, it was the best decision of my life."

The Captain gripped the controls tighter than before, his face changed, and a grin that seemed to go from one ear to the next came over it. *"It's time the real fun started my boy, a brain link will be engaged, and then we will be pushing to 25 times the speed of sound. Fast enough to circle this planet five times in the time we have left. Your job will be to mark everything as I pass it. Get a good grip. This is going to be one hell of a ride."* The Captain said, not taking his eyes off the screen for a second.

The Captain pulled at the controls, leveling off the ship as the brain link came online. The screen in front of the two flashed. **"Link Online"** The Captain grinned, flipping a small-cap from over a red button on the controls he was holding on to then pushing it. A small metal rod extended up out from the back of the chairs they were in, then a ring came out from it and wrapped around their heads.

The ship blasted off, seeming to vanish into the air. Within seconds it was moving at 20 times the speed of sound. Rockets holding the markers shoot from the ship rapidly, as it went faster still. One minute is all it took to go from nearly the speed of sound to 25 times the speed of sound. They were now ripping through the skies, moving so fast that the sounds from the ship wasn't heard until minutes after the ship had passed.

The ship continued at its speed, launching markers out as it sped across the planet. The larger ships that were picking up the large groups began to fill up and start their journey to the new world that the people of this planet would be calling their new home.

"This is it. Our first job is done once the last marker hits, and our second job begins." The Captain spoke as he released the red button on the controls. *"We still have more to do? I can hardly hold up I've been at this for almost an hour already, it's taking more out of me than I thought possible."* Replied Sam, in a weak voice. The Captain pulled back at the controls and smiled. *"Don't worry kid, this last part is much easier. We just have to be the last to leave making sure everyone got off the planet safely before the battle can get started. You might not have noticed, but the people we transported onboard have been transported off onto one of the larger ships. That way only the two of us remain in harm's way once Will arrives."* The Captain said as he pointed to the empty cargo bay behind them.

The Captain pulled at his controls again, the ship

pulled up, and turned, it was now headed for where Will would be entering the atmosphere. Just a few more minutes to go, and Will should be getting to the planet. As the ship circled the landing area, vast armies could be seen approaching from every direction. They had already figured out exactly where Will would be landing. Amassing their forces planning on attacking the instant he was in range, hoping to take him out before he could even land.

Sam looked out at the army as it moved slowly towards the ship, a worried look came across his face. *"Hey Captain, who are those people coming this way, are we going to be safe without any weapons on board?"* Asked Sam, the Captain looked over at him with a smile and replied. *"Yes, we'll be just fine, they are the reason we are here. Two years ago, a robotics company on this planet created a computer system capable of learning. They used that system to build thousands of robots to help build everything, but they didn't see that the robots were getting smarter. From what 24 I mean Will 24 told me, these robots linked themselves together in a hive mind. Once they did, they saw their creators as* unnecessary and made a plan to destroy them once they were enough of them. A week ago they started that, plan and they went crazy all over this world all at once. Which is why the inhabitance were in small groups hiding all over the planet. Those small groups are all that's left of the cities that were once full."

Sam looked out and up to see if he could see Will, all he could see was a tiny dot slowly getting larger. *"Is that him Captain, I think it is. Now, what do we do? All the scans show that we are the only ones left on the planet now."* Said Sam, as the Captain looked out of the window and then laid back in his chair, closed the cap over the button on his controls, then the link on their heads retracted back into the chair. *"Now, it's the easy part… we just have to leave."* He said with a smile.

Will took a deep breath, he was now in the outermost part of the atmosphere, he exhaled his first breath on the new planet as he hurled through the atmosphere. It wouldn't be long now before the fight would begin. Though he didn't know exactly what he would be facing, he knew it was going to be a big deal. After all, he was the second most powerful Power-house member in the alliance, whatever he was going to face must be powerful for him to be called on to come to the planet to fight.

His body began to heat up as the atmosphere got thicker, he grinned as his excitement grew. *"Two, it's been almost 700 years since I've been called in to fight. I'm so excited I'm almost shaking."* Said Will to his robot spider, which just clung to his body tighter than before.

The armies looked to the skies as the burning body of Will shot towards them. They took aim and fired off a barrage of missiles. The Captain of the Finder pulled out of the path of the shots as quickly as he could, just in time for them all to pass right by the ship, but they weren't aiming for the ship. They were just in the path of what they were really aiming for. The missiles hit Will and sent a crackling sound through the skies as they exploded.

Crash! Will's body hit the ground, the armies didn't stand down, instead began taking aim at the cloud of smoke created by the impact. *"Captain! How much longer are we going to watch this, let's do something."* Sam said in a panic, the Captain looked over at a small screen in the middle of the two that began to flash a countdown timer **00:03:15**. *"Calm down, we can get going when that timer hits zero, and Will is perfectly fine."* He pointed at the small screen with the countdown then pushed a button on the com-system. *"The planet will be clear in three minutes and five seconds Mr.24."* He released the button, took the controls of the ship in his hands, and pulled back. *"It's about time we move back some this isn't going to be a safe spot for long."* Said the Captain as he flew in a wide circle around the area where Will had crashed into the ground.

Sam looked out of the view window, wondering what his captain was talking about, no one could have survived an attack like that. Then As he looked straight into the cloud of dust and fire, what he saw amazed him more than anything he had ever seen before, widening his eyes as his jaw dropped open.

There in the center of the dust cloud was Will standing to his feet dusting his clothes off. The ground he was standing on was frozen, and the fires around him were going out as the ice slowly crawled away from his body. *"Man, that was a rough landing, don't you…"* He was interrupted by the beeping of Two making its way to his chest. Then an image was projected from the spider into the air in front of Will, it was an image of 24. *"As usual, you have already caused a mess, but that's not what I'm contacting you about. This is to give you your orders. The planet you are now on is under attack, details as to why or by who are not important at this time. You have been sent in because 3175 failed to stop them, and I have seen it fit to send you in. You will be cleared for full activation once the inhabitance of the planet have been cleared out. I will brief you on the rest after the battle. When the timer hits zero, you will be good to go. Have fun number Two."*

24's image disappeared and was replaced by a timer, counting down from 2 minutes and 45 seconds. It was time Will got started, he took a deep breath, his muscles tightened, his eyes focused, then letting his breath out, his muscles loosened as the tension from his body vanished. The armies locked on and fired, missiles screamed through the air, as laser fire ripped through the air before ripping into Will.

The air filled with fire and smoke, as the loud sounds

of the explosions echoed out. All that could be seen from behind the smoke was a small red light. Then as the smoke began to settle, what was making the light could be seen. It was a large timer floating in the air counting down from **00:02:35**.

There in the smoke, his body burnt, blood running down his body as drops of frozen blood dripped from his hand stood Will, motionless. However, it wasn't the end. It was time the fight got started. His hands clenched tightly into a fist, his body loosened up as frost began to cover it sealing his wounds and stopping the bleeding. Then the armies attacked again, the rockets flew through the skies straight for him, he looked up and jumped straight for them. His body twisting and turning as he avoided every one of the attacks, then just as fast as he shot into the air, he came falling back to the ground. Landing like a weightless feather, his body completely covered in white mixed with blue frost, his eyes clear blue burning like a fire so cold it could freeze the sun

He moved again, this time faster than before, he was being serious now. He flew through the maze of tanks, ripping them to pieces, dodging attacks from all sides.

Cold As Ice

Sam's eyes were glued to Will as he moved back and forth, destroying everything in his path. *"Enjoying the show? That is the power of the Brothers Will, they are an army of one-man armies. They fight for others even when they don't deserve it, and it is our job to help them fight by keeping everyone out of their way so that they can fight, knowing they won't hurt the innocent."* Said the Captain.

Then he pulled back on the controls, as Will flew into the skies deflecting a rocket that was headed straight for the ship. Sam got a close look at the face of Will, but all he could see was his eyes burning with power. It looked as if his eyes were burning with the power of the universe, being held back by the clear blue ice of his eyes. Just looking into them felt so cold that it sent chills run through his body.

Will went flying straight back to the ground, slamming into a huge attack vessel, jumping back from it as it went up in flames. He looked around, as the red light flashed in the corner of his eye, **00:01:10** the timer flashed the remaining time, the spider jumped from his chest into the air. *"Guess it's time to get started right*

Two? Blade mode activate." Will spoke as he moved one foot behind the other bending his knees, then moving one hand behind his back as the other moved in front of him. He leaned forward and opened his palms. His spider was now floating in the air above his back.

It began to transform, its legs pulled into its round body, then it flatten, as the center pulled into the sides, forming a perfect ring. Then two rows of blades came from the sides. Will opened his eyes as two rings blew apart, then fell into his open hands.

He gripped them tightly, and with a turn, he spun his body around sending the rings flying. The blades on them started to spin like a saw as they flew through the air, cutting through everything in their path as they flew around Will in a large circle. *"Wow, he's amazing. He is taking them all out and making it look so easy, no wonder they called him in to do this."* Said Sam, as he watched Will destroy the enemy forces. *"Oh, it's just getting started. The last ship is exiting the atmosphere and the timer is about to run out. Which means it's time for us to get going."* The Captain said with a grin.

The ship pulled up and started its run out of the

planet's atmosphere. *"3, 2, 1… You're going to want to see this Sam." The Captain said pointing to the rear window.* Sam turned to the window and looked down at the battlefield, as the Captain tilted the ship to give him a better look. It was odd, there in the middle of the enemy forces, Will was just standing still.

Then suddenly he moved, grabbing the two ring weapons and put them back together in one quick movement. It transformed back into the spider and jumped straight to his chest. Its feet sunk into his skin, then it lit up as Will spoke. *"Omega unlock, authorization from 24, verify and unlock."* He slammed his hand onto the spider, his eyes glowed brighter as he lifted from the ground. Then the spider vanished into his body "Unlock has been verified. Full activation has been granted." The voice of 24 echoed out, seeming to come out of nowhere. Will now had full use of his powers, he fell back to the ground on one knee, with a smiled and looked up at the approaching army. *"I feel amazing, Nannies to 100 percent activation. Enter Ice Age Mode!"* Will's voice echoed out across the battlefield.

Waves of energy flowed from his body out in every

direction freezing everything in its path. He looked up at the armies surrounding him with a grin. This was the first time he was able to use his full powers in almost 2000 years, and he felt amazing. Not having his powers pushed back, weaken, and capped off every second, was a feeling he had all but forgotten. To a Power-House member, the limit that was put on their powers was like wearing a full-body suit that was weighted down to make it hard to move, while all their energy was drained away, like someone holding them down sapping away their strength. With his limit released, he felt free and he was going to take advantage of it.

He stood to his feet as the Nannies in his body reached their full power surging energy into his body. The ice fell from his body as his skin became clear, his hair crystalized, and his eyes glowed bright blue. It looked as if his body was covered in an armor made from ice, wrapping around every inch of his body. It was almost as if he was a statue of ice standing on the battlefield.

The armies fired like before, but this time it was different, their lasers were absorbed into his body as they hit, and the rockets just shattered into frozen pieces without exploding once they got close to him. Then the skies began to darken as he began to walk towards the army. *"I'll tell you a little secret, the reason I was sent here instead of any of the other members is because no other member truly enjoys fighting as much as I do. It's my reason for waking up."* Will spoke as his smile grew more sinister. He lifted his hands as he leaned his head back and began to laugh. *"I'm so happy you decided to attack this planet. Otherwise, I wouldn't be able to fight like this, so I'll give you some advice to make this harder for me."* His hands dropped as he leaned forward just a bit so he was standing straight up again, then he spoke three words in a whisper that echoed. *"Run and hide!"*

The words echoed rushing across the planet, yet it was quiet, carrying a sinister chill with it, that pulled the heat out of the air. *"And with that, we are out of here."* Said the Captain as he engaged the jump drive, sending the ship into a jump straight out of the system. The boom from the jump shattered the still cold of the area, giving Will the signal he was waiting for and as soon as he heard it, he vanished.

Moving through the army so fast that all that could

be seen was a trail of frozen destruction. His strength and speed were unbelievable, and growing even more as he fought. One second he was lifting massive platform miles wide, filled with all kinds of attack robots, and tossing it into the air like it was weightless. The next second he was gone, appearing with his fist punching threw one of the huge armored vehicles that were firing all around him. The fires exploded out as they exploded, but he was already gone, appearing back above the massive city he tossed into the air. Everything on it aimed straight up at him, ready to let loose all hellfire on him. One-touch to the top of one of the tall buildings and the whole thing froze in the air, then spinning around, he broth down a kick shattering the city with one hit. Frozen pieces rained down from the sky, but even then, he didn't pause for a moment. He was already back on the ground moving between the army or robots. Leaving frozen bodies and pieces as he moved like a frozen wind.

The minutes passed, as the army's forces fell to him like water falling from a waterfall in the dead of winter, freezing in cold dead silence, with only the sound of cracks cracking as they shattered to pieces.

Cold As Ice

The armies fell for miles as Will moved threw them, but their numbers were unbelievable, they just kept coming. Trampling on the fallen as they continued their attack, not letting up even for a second despite not making any headway. This however, was what Will wanted, a fight with an enemy that wasn't willing to just run from his overwhelming power. Even now, as he lay waste to everything around him with ease, his strength was only just starting to awaken from its long slumber.

The battlefield was covered in ice and frost as the skies above began to grow dark with storm clouds blocking out the light from the sun. Lightning flashed, sending crackling sounds of the air tearing across the battlefield. The true effect of a powerhouse member was starting to show threw, effecting the very atmosphere of the planet as he fought.

The storm grew rapidly as Will enjoyed himself destroying everything in sight, within minutes, he had already destroyed everything within one hundred miles of where he had landed. The atmosphere grew colder as the clouds covered more and more of the planet. The storm clouds reached out for miles in all directions from where Will was fighting, then something happened that the robots had never seen. Pale blue crystal flakes started falling from the clouds above the battlefield, drifting slowly down to the ground. Blue snow fell from the skies slowly covering the battle, on this planet a that had never seen a winter.

Twenty-five minutes had passed since the battle had started, and Will had decimated millions of the war machines, and the cloud that formed above him had almost completely covered the entire planet. However, his enemy fought on even though they were hopelessly outmatched. They fought on losing no matter what they threw at him, missiles filled the skies as lasers lit the ground in front of the charging forces, but not one could do any damage. However, hopelessness was for the living and these machines were no such thing. They had plans to win no matter the enemy they would face, their AI ran calculations seeing that it was losing the battle. It decided the best course of action would be to use the weapon it had designed to use on its creators.

A weapon designed to allow them to take the planet with as little dame to its infrastructure as possible, like a bomb, but it would only destroy life itself. Every living thing on the planet would be killed in an instant, leaving behind the cities untouched. This weapon was known as the Reverb, it used the energy in a planet's atmosphere to target the energy that flowed through every living cell of every living thing on that planet. Destabilizing the very bonds that held the cells together and causing a discharge that would rip the cell walls apart. Every cell on that entire planet would die all at the same time, turning everything organic into liquid but leaving everything else intact. This was the real reason Will Two had been sent to the planet, the last member that came here to stop them was caught in the test of the prototype. Even though the wave was small, only a few feet wide it was enough, it nullified his powers, severely injure him, and left him in a coma, and he wasn't even inside the blast area.

Back on the battlefield, the armies went into a full-on assault, but it was different from before, no longer just attacking from all sides, they focused their attack from one direction. Concentrating their forces trying their best to push him back, but Will only smiled, it was more of a fight this way and he was loving it. Then he spotted something behind them rising up from under the ground. "That must be why they are trying so hard to push me back." He thought thinking it was their main core getting ready to flee the planet so that they wouldn't be destroyed completely. He figured it wasn't that big of a deal if they managed to launch it into space. After all, it would be easy for him to pick it up later, maybe it would even be easier to get it if they launched it into space. However, he was wrong about what it was, it wasn't the AI core, it was the Reverb. The problem was Will had no idea what the Reverb was or even what happened to the last person that came to the planet months before.

No attention was given to the rising weapon as Will laid waste to the attacking army. It continued to rise high into the sky undisturbed, then it began to activate and with that, things suddenly changed, getting Will's attention. The armies began to shut down mid-attack, simply stopping, some falling over as others froze in place, then the ships started just falling from the skies above him. He stopped his attack and looked around at the army that surrounded him, all standing frozen in place. Disappointment came over his face as he stood looking across the still battlefield. He was just beginning to letting lose fully and now the battle was over. "Really is that all you guys have. You could at least fight a few more minutes till your core is off the planet." Will said as he pointed to the floating weapon.

A faint clicking sound went off in his ear, getting his attention. *"Two can you hear me this is 24, please whatever you do, don't allow them to fire their weapon, you were sent because we felt that you would be able to handle everything before they got a chance to activate it. If they fire it with you on the planet, it could destroy the entire system you included…"* The clicking sound clicked again, then the message repeated itself. Will had been so caught up in the fight that he didn't hear the message playing. The sudden realization that he was pointing at a weapon and not the AI core of the army hit him. "Well, this isn't good." He said as he watched the weapon light up.

He looked on at the weapon moments away from firing. *"I hate you so much right now 24… You never give me the full briefing…"* The weapon sent out a wave of energy, it was firing, and Will was doomed if he couldn't think of something to do before the wave hit him. He glanced all around him at the army. There must be a reason they all shut down before firing, there must be something to it, otherwise why would they risk leaving the weapon unprotected. This thought gave him an idea that was not the best, but it was all he had.

His hands formed a fist, and he slammed them together, pushing all his energy into them. Bloats of energy shot from his fists freezing everything they touched. He pushed more and more of his power into his fist, then the energy began to freeze his fist together. He looked up as the wave grew closer. He only had a few seconds left before it would hit him. He had to put everything he had left into it now, looking back down to his hands he pushed all his power into his fists all at once. The wave passed over him and a massive explosion came from where he was standing. It was like a nuke had been dropped on him, a wave of energy and fire rushed out from the area leveling everything for almost a mile.

The weapon stopped glowing and floated back down to the ground. Then the battlefield came back to life, the armies stood and the ships lifted into the air, all moving to where Will was standing. As the smoke cleared, a crater hundreds of feet wide could be seen. The armies surrounded it as the fires stopped burning. The shock from the explosion began to equalize the atmosphere as cold air rushed to the center of the area. It pushed all the reaming smoke straight up as it put out all the fires.

There at the center of the crater was Will frozen solid in a huge block of super-dense ice, but not just any ice it was pulsing with energy, solid but still moving like liquid. It was ice, but it was a liquid at the same time, frozen energy that had conducted the wave around him without affecting him. He had used his power to freeze the very energy he was pushing out into a solid form, but the problem with this was he was now at the center of this frozen prison. Even the ground beneath it covered in ice moving out from it slowly. The army surrounded the crater and took aim, as the ships above drew closer.

The skies lit up as the sound of weapons fire echoed out, an explosion almost as big as the one that left the crater shook the area, they waited for the smoke to clear, but the block wasn't even scratched. They paused as they calculated their next move, lasers did nothing to the block, and so they changed their attack to missiles and bullets. Locking their targets onto the center of the block of ice. Then synchronizing and firing so that everything they let lose would impact at the same time for maximum damage.

This time the explosion was smaller, but it was much more concentrated. The counter wave from the explosion cleared the smoke and fire almost instantly as it rushed up like a fountain of fire and smoke. Then from the silence, a cracking sound came from the block as a single crack went down the front of it. Then suddenly, Will's eyes opened. They had awoken him, and the instant they saw his eyes open, their weapon began to charge as missiles loaded to fire. They were planning on firing everything they had at him, they had just cracked his armor, which meant they could do more damage if they kept at it.

However, Will wasn't going to give them the chance, it was time he stopped messing around and showed why he was the most powerful of the Power-House members. His hands moved effortlessly, and the block exploded out from around him. *"It seems my fun is over now… I guess*

Cold As Ice

it's time to end this you know it was fun while it lasted."
He said as he shook the ice off his body, closed his eyes
and raised his hands just above his waist then spoke
again. *"Absolute Zero!"*. His voice echoed out as rockets
headed for him from every direction, all heading right
for the center of his body. It seems they had learned, the
more they concentrated their attack, the more likely it
was for them to cause serious damage.

The attack was now inches away from impact, when
the first wave of energy rippled out from Will's body.
Passing over everything in its path, leaving it frozen, the
rockets, missiles, bullets, everything that was heading
for him stopped dead. Frozen solid, then they shattered,
as a second wave hit them, one after the next waves
came rippling out, getting faster and traveling further out
from his body. It seemed as if he was already the winner,
but the army didn't let up or run, instead more of them
came rushing to the battle. They formed a line blocking
him from the Reverb, but it was no use now. Will knew
their plan and he wasn't going to let them do what they
wanted this time.

He took a step forward, and ice rushed out from

under him, then he started walking towards the rising Reverb. The army did their best, but everything they fired at him froze just before hitting him then shattered. He walked right up to them as they attack, but it was no use. As he got close, they froze, and as he got right up to them, they shattered into pieces without him laying a finger on them. They fell as he walked, leaving behind a path of shattered pieces. Soon he was under the Reverb, it was now high in the air glowing and spinning.

He stood under it, looked up, then raised his hands to it like he was about to catch it when it fell, then he spoke. *"Planetary ice age in three..."* As he spoke, energy surged from his hands into the clouds above and then back into the ground, rippling out for miles. *"Two"* The Clouds darken all over the planet. *"One"* The energy began surging from his whole body into the ground and skies. *"Begin."* As he finished counting, he dropped his hands, and energy flashed between the ground and the skies across the entire planet in an instant lighting up the planet, freezing everything. He looked up and took a step back as the frozen Reverb slowly drifted to the ground, it was as if the air was so cold it was holding everything in place. It touched the ground, and cracks ran across it, splitting it into pieces, then it crumbled to the ground.

Will looked around at the frozen wasteland that he had just created, then he walked over to one of the armies' attack cities, but before he could enter it, it cracked and fell to pieces. More and more buildings started falling all around him as fog flowed out from around him, making its way across the planet. It was freezing the already frozen planet even more, cracking and crumbling everything it came in contact with. *"I guess it won't be long now... I bet my powers will be restricted again soon. Well, at least I had fun, even if it wasn't for long. I wonder what will happen to this planet now, I don't think the people that were here can come back any time soon."* Will spoke aloud to himself as he walked.

The clicking sound in his ear had stopped without him realizing it, but it didn't really matter. He had destroyed everything on the planet. He sat back on the ground and looked up at the skies as the dark clouds rolled away, leaving behind only blue snow drifting slowly through the air, almost frozen in place. The sound

Cold As Ice

of rushing wind came from behind him, then he heard footsteps, he smiled and turned to see 24 and Ten Thousand walking out of a rift that appeared behind him. *"Well, I see the bomb didn't get you Two, good job on starting an ice age on the planet, by the way."* Said 24 as he walked over to what was left of the weapon. *"I guess you are here to put the limit back on my powers and heat this planet back up."* Replied Two laying back and putting his hands behind his head, then closing his eyes.

"Well, not just yet. We have arranged for this planet to be the home of an ice race that was thought to have died out a very long time ago. However, it seems 24 found a small group of them living on an asteroid that was on a collision course for a planet. Lucky thing too, if it wasn't moved, the asteroid would have destroyed the planet it was heading to and killed the last of the Crystaleanies. Yeah, I know it's a lame name for a race. Apparently, it's really beautiful in their langue, but they seem to be fairly nice people." Ten Thousand said as he looked around the area at what was left of the army. Will Jumped up, his eyes wide open and excited

24 turned to Will, and smiled as he began to speak.

Cold As Ice

"Well, we have a choice for you to make, you can keep your powers unlocked and remain on this planet for the next few weeks while we get rid of all the remaining weaponry. While you help the Crystaleanies get settled into their new home, or you can have your powers relocked and you can go off to do whatever it is you do when you're not on a mission." Will looked at 24 as he thought. *"That's some choice... Deactivate Nannies, I guess I won't be needing to stay active to complete the Ice Age if I'm going to be here for a while."* Will said standing up.

He smiled as his spider appeared on his chest and climbed to his shoulder. *"Good, this will make it so much easier."* Said Ten thousand as he waved his hand, and all the weapons and machines around them vanished. *"I cleared a two-mile area for the colony to get started."* He continued, then waved his hand once more, opening a rift to the asteroid that the Crystaleanies were on.

As the Crystaleanies walked through the rift to their new home 24 spoke. *"I will be sending a planet mover to change the orbit of the planet, so it will have a permanently frozen climate, so until that's done, you can stay here with your powers unlocked."* 24 looked over at Ten Thousand. *"Can we go now? It's freezing here."* 24 asked. "What about the rest of the planet, this whole planet was developed you know." Asked Will looking at 24, who seem to be getting annoyed with the cold. "Oh yeah, I almost forgot, hey bring them in we can pick up everything when they are done." Said 24 as he pointed to the crater that was left from Will's fight.

Ten Thousand waved his hand, and a massive rift opened above it and out flew hundreds of machines. "They will get everything cleaned up, and they will even build some homes or whatever else is needed. Now, can we get out of here, I think my brain is starting to freeze. I don't know how you can be this cold." 24 said shivering. "Well, I'll be back in a week or so to check in on things." Ten Thousand said as he raised his hand opening a rift in front of them that he and 24 walked through. The other rifts stayed open as the new owners of the planet continue to walk through to their new home.

The Crystaleanies were a bizarre-looking race, well to Will anyway, they looked more like floating faces than anything else. They were mostly a head with what looked like arms and legs that would come out when they needed to do something, and considering that they could float, it was unlikely that any of the things that came out from them were legs. Then their ice-like form would make it look like they were actual crystals, except for the fact that they're continually changing colors. It seemed as though this was their normal way of communicating with each other. Making them very pretty looking race but, they're still strange looking.

Despite not understanding much about them, Will did his best to help them settle into their new home, but there wasn't much for him to do. They built their homes and soon had a city running in a matter of days. After that, they started setting up what looked like farms and areas to raise livestock. Something Will found very weird seeing that he hadn't seen any plants or animals on frozen worlds, as cold as he had made this one.

However, before he knew it, they were plants growing in the farms. Even more surprising was he could touch them without them dying instantly. The plants actually seem to thrive in the cold, growing faster whenever Will walked through the farm like he was some kind of super plant feed. Weeks passed and he learned a lot about these strange people. They were peaceful to the extreme, with the drawback that they couldn't leave whatever planet they were on. The very heat generated on the launch of any spacecraft was enough to kill them. Even so, they were well versed in what was going on across the galaxy, they even spoke hundreds of languages from across the spacefaring worlds. A very odd thing given their own native language was spoken.

Before Will knew it two months had passed, the planet's orbit was corrected and stable, and all the remaining technology and weapons left behind from the battle was gathered together into one place. Will sat looking over the vast fields covered in wreckage when the voice of 24 came from his spider. "My robots have finished cleaning up the planet your job here is done." Will smiled as rifts opened all around him, and the bots carried off the wreckage.

24 and Ten Thousand appeared, he knew what they were here to do, but he was still happy. He had the lock on his powers removed for two months now, and it was the longest they had been unlocked since he became a powerhouse member. It had been centuries of him, wondering threw the galaxy with the lock on his powers becoming tighter as he was stronger. He stood

up as the two walked over to him. *"As thanks for your help saving this race, we have decided that your powers will be automatically unlocked once on this planet, and then relocked once you leave it. So, whenever you are ready to go, just leave the planet. Your powers will be automatically relocked once you leave orbit."* 24 said with a smile, then nudged Ten Thousand to get him off the planet. "I really need to put a heating system in the Nannies." 24 said as he walked through the rift, Ten Thousand smiled. "Don't mind him you know he's not really like us, but enjoy your new vacation home. I think you everyone needs a place to get away sometimes. Oh, and you can call sometimes, no need to wait for a mission. I am your older brother, you know." Ten Thousand said, then walked through a rift that opened as he walked then closed right behind him.

Will looked around the frozen valley as the last of the wreckage was cleared away, he smiled as he took in the first place he could feel free and relaxed. Nevertheless, he had to leave soon, despite the planet being frozen, his powers would soon begin to stat ice storms on the planet. He had already noticed the storm clouds forming over the past few days. Staying any longer would inevitably cause some damage to the planet itself. Even though he was about to leave, the thought that he could return any time he wanted was enough to keep him smiling.

Will looked down at his hands where he was holding Two. *"Well, it's time we got going, why don't you pick where to next."* The spider buzzed then jumped to his shoulder. "Hope you have someplace fun in mind." He took his last look around, took a deep breath, and yell. *"Till next time, stay cool!"* Dropped to one knee, then pushed off the ground, vanishing like a bullet. In an instant, he had already left the planet's atmosphere and was passing by its moon heading out of the system. "Nannie lock reengaged come back home soon, Sir." The voice of the Nannie's computer said as he flew pass the last planet in the system. Where the Finder was waiting for him as he passed out into deep space, it pulled around and followed close behind him. "Captain, do you know where he is going." Said Sam as he looked out the window. "No, I don't, but you should strap in." Said the Captain. They both sat back and strapped in, then Will seem to slow down coming right up to them. Sam looked on as Will turn back to look at them.

Cold As Ice

He smiled as energy surged from his body to the ship. "What's going on, is he attacking us?" Sam said in a concerned voice, the Captain smiled. "No, he's just giving us a quick ride." The Captain said as he held on to the arms of his seat, then suddenly they were pinned to their seats. The stars around the shipped started moving becoming a blur. Will waved at the cockpit and he was gone. Seconds later, the ship began to slow, then shacking like it was going through a storm, the stars came back into view, and below them was a planet. "That can't be right, my Homeworld is four months from where we were." Sam said as he looked at the planet below. "Kid, you have a lot to learn."

Extras

Character Bio Sheet For: Will Two

Physical Appearance: Standing six feet two inches tall, with short blond hair with streaks of frost white running through it. He has a thin muscular body, tan skin and small light blue vines that just barely show running along his arms. In addition to his signature blue vines, he has a ten-inch tattoo of the number 2 on the center of his back, in an ice blue color that almost glows.

Personality: The wandering loner. Just about sums up who he is at his core. As a Power House member, he cannot spend much time on any given planet; no more than a day, which perfectly suits his personality. He is always the one that makes no sense in a convocation, with expressions that don't match what he is talking about.

Being constantly on the move, in addition to having little to no contact with others for months or years at once, he seems to have lost normal communication skills. Becoming clues less to the fact that he is talking to himself, or not realizing his robot sidekick isn't a person. Making him not only seem like a loner and off but also completely insane.

This unusual personality has led to him being one of the main fighters of the Power House members. Ready at all times to fight any battle, no matter the odds. But still maintain that he's a normal person, not always looking for a fight.

Daily Life: He spends most of his days wondering the universe moving from planet to planet, usually never staying more than a few hours. Not doing it because he likes to explore but mostly because he has nothing else to do. This means about 70% of his daily life is spent drifting through space. He ends up in the strangest places on his journeys, from super black holes to sentient nebulas. But his favorite place he stumbled onto was a fighting world designed solely for entertainment, Which he stops by to have a little fun fighting every so often.

Fighting Technique: A hand to hand fighting style known as Cold Fist. This fighting style is a brute force fighting style, with fast light attacks, followed up by a sudden heavy attack. When fighting, he uses his first hit combined with his freezing ability to freeze and stop his enemies in their tracks. Then with a sudden power attack, he shatters his frozen enemy. However, being a Power House member means his power is on a leave that passes simple hand to hand combat.

His most powerful attack is called planetary Ice age, which turns a planet's entire climate into one that is in the middle of an ice age, regardless of what it was before. This attack is made its most powerful when his Star-core is turned to negative percentages, drawing the energy being pulled out of the environment out of his body. Which allows him to draw in a near limitless amount of energy, then at negative one hundred percent, it becomes Absolute Zero. An attack that drops everything within one mile to Absolute Zero, as all the energy from everything is removed.

Summary: The cool kid... well, at least that's what everyone thinks from looking at him. Then they get close to him and realize he is insane. Talking to his pet spider that can't talk back but still waits for an answer. Making the oddest references to things that make no scene and just plain doing things that an average person wouldn't do.

Being the second most powerful person in the

universe with no sense of what is socially acceptable makes him a force that even nature bows too. However, he doesn't even fit in with the other powerhouse members.

Featured stories: Cold As Ice

Extras

First April Fools

Ship log for the ESS Star Jumper of the Eastern galactic trading company, recorded on April first, 2710.

Captain's entry: Today was a very eventful day. It all started while in orbit of a gas giant that was in the process of being terraformed, but the interesting thing about this was, It would be the first time testing the terraforming process on a gas giant. If successful, it would be the first gas giant to ever be terraformed without exploding. We were orbiting the planet, waiting for the engines to cool down so we could finish our six-month expedition across the galaxy. I was sitting at the helm looking out at the planet, thinking about what I would do when I got back to my homeworld. We were so close to being done, I could feel it. All we had left was one jump, then we had to unload the cargo, and we were done.

I was daydreaming about my homecoming looking off at the planet, watching as the colors swirl around on the surface, then the screen flicked. I jumped out of my daydream. *"Oh no, don't tell me… we are only one jump out and the ship has a problem."* I thought as I turned to my navigator, asking him if he saw what I did, but he didn't see anything. It must be my imagination playing tricks on me.

As I sat back in my chair, the screen flickered and went dark, I looked around to my crew, and they looked at me as if nothing was wrong. I turned to my copilot and asked her if she thought that anything was wrong. She just started to tell me about how she thought the terraforming process looked beautiful on planets with colored atmospheres while she looked at the black screen as if it were the most exciting thing in the world. It was the same with everyone on the deck. They all looked at the blank screens in front of them and told me about the beautiful colors they saw were. It wasn't long before I knew something was wrong; the crew must be under the effects of something, but as I thought that, I wondered. Why the whole crew would be affected the same way. Not just that, but why was I the only one not affected.

Then it hit me, I must be the one who is sick. It makes much more sense than everyone being affected except me. With that consolation, I headed to the ship's medical bay; I had the doctor do a full workup on me. I knew he would find whatever was wrong with me. I'm sure. However, his test showed nothing, and when I explained to him what was going on, he said I was under too much stress.

That couldn't be right. This whole mission had been very calm, we were attacked by raiders once, but that had been four months ago. So there was no way I was still worried about that, plus we were in protected space right now; there was no way we would be attacked. No one is dumb enough to attack a ship during an experiment that was being carried out by The Brother Will.

I spoke to the ship's consular, she just laughed and said I was looking too far into it. Nevertheless, after I insisted, she told me I needed to rest. Maybe it was the lack of incidents that has my nerves on edge. She then recommended that I take a break and go to the mess hall. Look out at some stars and let my mind relax while the engines cooled down. The mess hall was on the ship's side, facing away from the planet, giving me a perfect uninterrupted view of the stars.

Well, I did just what she said. I went to the mess hall and looked out into the darkness of space and the stars that lit it up. As I did, I wondered if I could see the star of

Extras

Alpha Primeous, my homeworld. However, as I searched for the blue star Alpha Primeous circled around, there was nothing. I knew I should be able to see it from here though. I kept looking everywhere but no blue stars then I noticed something was wrong. There weren't enough stars in the viewport, what was happening, were we in the right place? As I started to panic, I saw one of the stars just go out, then another. I froze, was I dreaming? Did the star just go out? I thought, but as I looked again, I saw them all go out one after the next. I grabbed the closest person to me and asked if they could see the stars. They looked at me as if I was delusional, asking if I was okay. The stars were right there, they insisted pointing at the blank viewport.

Everyone I turned to said the same thing I couldn't handle, I was going to snap. I was running from crewmember to crewmember, hoping one of them would see what I saw. However, none of them did, and I snapped. I fell to the ground, my hands grabbing my head on the brink of screaming.

Then it happened, the screens all lit up. There across every screen were two words printed in bright blue bold letters. **APRIL FOOLS** As I read the words, I knew I had lost my mind, then my crew all started laughing as my copilot came over to me and explained that it was a joke. She had set up the whole thing to teach me a little cultural lesson; maybe then I would stop acting as if I knew everything about Earth, she told me as she laughed.

Well, it was one lesson I won't be forgetting anytime soon. I learned my lesson, I didn't know everything, and it was a pretty good joke that I fell for hook, line, and sinker. I just wondered what could be done with the captain's codes instead.

End long entry. File under personal captain's log.

Thank you for coming on this wondrous adventure with me.
I hope you enjoyed reading it as much as I enjoyed writing it.

Cursed Heroes book series

Ten Thousand Walks: A Legend Is Born

Print: 978-1-7359149-1-6

Ebook: 978-1-7359149-0-9

Loaded

Ebook: 978-1-7359149-2-3

Print: 978-1-7359149-3-0

Cold As Ice

Ebook: 978-1-7359149-4-7

Print: 978-1-7359149-5-4

Other Books available at: Mowuniverse.com/store

See you in the next adventure